PIECES

"LÉO TRÉZENIK" was the pseudonym assumed Léo Épinette (1855-1902). He was a French poet, novelist and journalist who, in 1883, cofounded the literary journal *Lutèce*, the first periodical explicitly associated with "Symbolist" poetry, publishing, among many others, the works of Paul Verlaine. Among his works are *Proses décadentes* (1886), *L'abbé Coqueluche* (1889), and *La Confession d'un fou* (1890).

BRIAN STABLEFORD'S scholarly work includes *New Atlantis: A Narrative History of Scientific Romance* (Wildside Press, 2016), *The Plurality of Imaginary Worlds: The Evolution of French roman scientifique* (Black Coat Press, 2017) and *Tales of Enchantment and Disenchantment: A History of Faerie* (Black Coat Press, 2019). In support of the latter projects he has translated more than a hundred volumes of *roman scientifique* and more than twenty volumes of *contes de fées* into English.

His recent fiction, in the genre of metaphysical fantasy, includes a trilogy of novels set in West Wales, consisting of *Spirits of the Vasty Deep* (2018), *The Insubstantial Pageant* (2018) and *The Truths of Darkness* (2019), published by Snuggly Books.

SNUGGLY BOOKS

LÉO TRÉZENIK

DECADENT PROSE PIECES

TRANSLATED AND WITH AN INTRODUCTION BY

BRIAN STABLEFORD

THIS IS A SNUGGLY BOOK

ISBN: 978-1-64525-028-9

CONTENTS

INTRODUCTION

*P*ROSES DÉCADENTES by "Léo Trézenik"
(Léo Épinette, 1855-1902), was originally
published by E. Girard et Cie at the Imprimerie
de *Lutèce* in 1886. It was one of the first volumes to
advertise itself brazenly as a contribution to a nascent
Decadent Movement, albeit ironically and in jest—an
irony and humor entirely appropriate to the spirit of
the school in question.

Trézenik had joined Émile Goudeau's Hydropathes
Club in the days when its meetings were held at the
Chat Noir, and he soon took on a prominent role in the
association. After some preliminary ventures in journal-
ism he formed an association with Charles Morice to
transform the anticlerical revue *La Nouvelle Rive Gauche*
into the literary periodical *Lutèce* in 1883. *Lutèce*, the
contributors to which included Paul Verlaine, Jean
Moréas and Jules Laforgue, became the first periodical
explicitly associated with "Symbolist" poetry, although
its promoters had not yet wholly embraced that label,
let alone the supplementary label "Decadent," which
quickly came to be applied to it, initially as a criti-

cism. The latter accusation was, however, immediately adopted by some of its proponents, in imitation of Charles Baudelaire, who had long ago embraced the intended insult when it was aimed at Romanticism and had construed it perversely as a compliment. Trézenik and his collaborators appreciated that irony fully, and made the most of it in their own commentaries.

In particular, Trézenik appreciated the role played by popularizing the two labels by a literary hoax to which several of the newspapers of the day fell victim. A collection of parodic poems entitled *Les Déliquescences d'Adoré Floupette* (1885), concocted by Henri Beauclair and Gabriel Vicaire,[1] with a biographical preface signed "Marius Tapora" advertised itself as both Symbolist and Decadent, and more than one newspaper critic accepted it as a significant contribution to an emerging phenomenon. In the prefatory note to his own collection, Trézenik advertises it as a companion of sorts to that parody, reflecting the important role played in the new fashion by brief prose vignettes, often labeled oxymoronically as "poems in prose"—a format that many of his contemporaries had adopted eagerly, following in the tracks of Baudelaire. The preface tacitly suggests to

---

1 Henri Beauclair (1860-1919) was a journalist and habitué of Le Chat Noir who worked for numerous publications, including *Lutèce*, before becoming editor of the daily newspaper *Le Petit Journal* in 1906. He had a particular flair for satire. He recruited the older and more prestigious poet Gabriel Vicaire (1848-1900), who had a typically Hydropathic fondness for writing drinking songs, to help him concoct the poems of Adoré Floupette, available in English translation from Atlas Press as *The Deliquescences of Adoré Floupette: Decadent Poems* (2007).

readers that the contents of the collection need not be taken seriously, but leaves it to them to make up their own minds as to the extent of double bluff there might be in that advertisement.

Decadent literature was, at its very inception in mid-century, replete with black comedy, essentially playful and provocative in its self-indulgent perversity and licentiousness. An element of parody is intrinsic to it, but it is not always appreciated; a great deal has been written about the book that came to be regarded as the cardinal example of Decadent prose, Joris-Karl Huysmans, *À rebours* (1884), of which a surprising amount ignores the fact that it is a comedy, a fantasy of exaggeration. The same is true of Huysmans' prose vignettes, collected in *Le Drageoir aux épices* (1874) and *Croquis parisiens* (1880), which likewise came to be seen retrospectively as crucial contributions to the revitalization of the "prose poem" and its particular association with a revived literary "decadence." When Huysmans suggested that the prose poem was "the osmazome of literature" he was not being entirely serious, but nor was he simply being silly.

Huysmans' prose pieces have much in common with Trézenik's collection, which is, on average, lighter in tone, but not sufficiently to be regarded simply as a caricature. Baudelaire wanted to call the collection of prose vignettes that he did not manage to publish during his lifetime as *Spleen de Paris*, and Trézenik's collection is both very Parisian and distinctly splenetic; its light touch is that of a steely forefinger. Trézenik explicitly sets his work up in opposition to the determined seriousness of Stéphane Mallarmé's school of Symbolism, but not in a destructive way or in an attempt to belittle it. Trézenik's collaborator Charles Morice was a theorist of Symbolism just as intellectually earnest as Mallarmé, entirely sympathetic to the use of symbolism in expressing and representing woe and distress as well as analyzing notions of beauty, but like Mallarmé, he did not deplore its use in more lighthearted projects, and he was sufficiently sensitive to the esthetics of the incongruous and the grotesque to make common cause with the more whimsical Trézenik. Although the idea of a collection of *Proses décadentes* would probably suggest to most readers an expression of lapidary style equipped with a sense of reverence, and many such collections did indeed embrace pretentions of that sort—Remy de Gourmont's *Proses moroses* (1894) is a classic example—there is no essential contradiction in the notion of a set of humorous Decadent prose pieces, well equipped to sustain the proverbial proposition that there is many a true word spoken in jest that is difficult to voice more politely.

It is worth remembering that the same cafés that spawned to Goudeau's Hydropathes also played host, simultaneously, to Jules Lévy and his fellow promoters of the Salon des Arts Incohérents, a significant precursor of Dadaism. The annual salon, usually accompanied by a masked ball, was launched in 1883, and the endeavor overlapped considerably with the literary endeavors hatched in the Chat Noir. Trézenik was the promoter of a partly-imaginary group that he called the Hirsutes [Hairy Ones], whose history and manifesto he serialized in *Lutèce* in 1883, and he was by no means the most extreme of the neo-Decadent writers who took aboard some of the ideology of the Incoherent Arts and incorporated it into their work; the short prose pieces published by Jules Laforgue, another prominent contributor to *Lutèce*, are considerably more incoherent and provocative, deliberately bordering on farce. The fact that Trézenik's prose pieces have a strong element of humor, therefore, certainly does not reduce the entire endeavor to trivial pastiche. The vignettes are, in fact, exemplary in their Decadence precisely because of a certain lack of delicacy. They are fully entitled to be juxtaposed with the prose poems of Charles Morice; the latter are more polished and more pretentious, but Trézenik's down-to-earth style has a commendable briskness that does not lose by the comparison.

The original of the present collection has been largely ignored by literary historians, perhaps because the preface was a little too extravagant in likening it so closely to the Floupette hoax, deterring commentators from the risk of being caught out by a deception. *Proses décadentes* is certainly humorous, but there is no more deception about it than is routine in the black-edged comedy intrinsic to the skeptical perversity of decadent philosophy. Trézenik was an important pioneer of the *fin-de-siècle* Decadent Movement, in his own work as well as his editorial promotion, and the body of that work is considerable, including three novels, of which the most enterprising is the surreal *Confessions d'un fou* (1890), as well as his poetry and criticism. He is an underrated writer whose work deserves to be better known and more keenly appreciated.

The translation was made from the copy of the Girard edition reproduced on the Bibliothèque Nationale's *gallica* website.

—Brian Stableford

DECADENT
PROSE
PIECES

BY WAY OF A PREFACE

I wrote this in *Lutèce* on 16 August 1886:

Today that prejudice can no longer be borne against Floupette or its publisher; when *Les Déliquescences* have had the rare good fortune of making a tour of the major press and extracting from the dailies, always so miserly with their lines, a renown that no literary work as bold, sincere and savory has ever attained before; today, when after all the others—after Mermeix,[1] who did not understand it at all, after Claretie, who sensed its advent, and Arène, who approved of it in a smiling article, Paul Bourde, in the

---

1 "Mermeix" was the signature employed by the political journalist Gabriel Terrail (1859-1930). The other three commentators named are the littérateurs Jules Claretie and Paul Arène, both of whom must have been glad to participate in the joke, and the political journalist Paul Bourde (1851-1914), most famous for his jingoistic promotion of colonial enterprises, although his article in *Le Temps* on 6 August 1885 attacking the "decadence" of Stéphané Mallarmé and Paul Verlaine played an ironic leading role in establishing the label, exactly as Desiré Nisard had done half a century before, helping to make Jean Moréas' *Symbolist Manifesto* sufficiently newsworthy to warrant publication and promotion in *Le Figaro* in 1886.

grave *Le Temps*, worthy sheep of Panurge that he is, has chronicled the "Decadent School"; today, finally and in brief, when the joke has gone on long enough and is beginning to smell rancid, it is perhaps not unhelpful to reduce that floupetterie to its just proportions.

Already, in Tuesday's *Dixneuvième Siècle* (its editor presumably wanted to pass a sponge over the enormous gaffe initially committed with regard to Floupette by one of his finest reporters, Monsieur Mermeix) Moréas obligingly set out to demonstrate to Monsieur Bourde, personally, the extent to which he had been ill-informed in writing his article.

But that is insufficient. The entire press had been fooled in too resounding a fashion for it to be unnecessary to make it the belated but obligatory confidence that it has been the victim of a practical joke.

For, not only does Floupette not exist—this is still for the benefit of Monsieur Mermeix—but the Decadent School is an invention of Floupette, and his *Déliquescences* are not a parody but a fake genre created wholesale for his personal usage by the said Floupette.

For a start, the label "decadent," which it has pleased reporters, in the wake of Floupette, to level at young writers, is meaningless. Only Monsieur Prud'homme—although it is just to say that he contributes under many pseudonyms to the majority of the major Parisian newspapers—has the right to propose that Art is presently in decadence. There is no more "decadence" today than there was when "classical" Art attempted to replace Romanticism, when Hugo dethroned Ponsard; when, in 1830, *Les Burgraves* was acclaimed to the detriment of *Lucrèce*.[1] There was a simple transformation. There is a tendency of young literature to claim to be new, and for that reason to claim to be different. Labels signify nothing, to such an extent that the so-called decadents had already been labeled "neo-Romantics," because "Romanticism," fundamentally, at the time of its glory and audacity, only meant "change." And it is still Romanticism today, but neo-Romanticism trying to emerge in literary terms from the routine and the hidebound.

That, apart from two or three employees of Monsieur Mallarmé's "Art is Everything" bureau, is what the present-day literary Pleiad has attempted. That is what Monsieur Bourde has not understood. Because he has made up his entire article without reading twenty lines of each of the young poets about whom he perorates; because, like the worthy dullard and naïve critic he is, he has taken seriously the preface of "Marius Tapora," who had amused himself by magnifying, in jest, in order to poke fun at their pretensions, the personality of a few café rhymers, whom the morphinism of one and the Byzantine affectations of another had made sufficiently ridiculous for Beauclair, excellent parodist that he is, to be able to tell them so, once and for all.

The target being small, Beauclair, in order for it to be visible and so that no one should be astonished that

---

1 Victor Hugo's failed historical play *Les Burgraves*, produced in 1843, was swiftly followed by François Ponsard's classical tragedy *Lucrèce*, which was hailed by some critics as a revitalization of the obsolete tradition that had supposedly ended in 1830, when Hugo's *Hernani* had caused a sensation and had been loudly hailed as the beginning of a new Romantic era in the French theater.

he was amusing himself shooting at it, was constrained to exaggerate: an optical effect by which the press was duped. As the booklet, in itself, was merry, people laughed. Some of them laughed all the more loudly because they had not understood a treacherous word of it but wanted their neighbors to believe that they had understood it. That explains the improbable success that *Les Déliquescences* enjoyed.

That is all well and good.

I have nothing to add except that it is for that reason that I have entitled these fantasies *Proses décadentes*.

—Léo Trézenik

ON ADULTERY

SILENT for a long time, and strewn here and there in the room where she is asleep, the Adulteress, enlaced with Him in the hollow of a great calm bed with convulsed sheets; in the somnolent room that has even killed the rhythmic pulse of the clock, now, under the electric nickeling of the Moon, the Things—the disquieting Things that "want to keep their secret"—suddenly begin to talk among themselves.

The Stockings have begun, the delicate black silk stockings, empty now and collapsed at the foot of the long mocking sofa.

The Stockings said:

"It's because of us that he loved her. It's us who, molding her plump twins and their slender ankles ignited the gleam in his gaze that set fire to his soul."

And at length, in the silence of the night, the Stockings, the delicate Stockings sang, under the electric nickeling of the Moon, the unforgettable poem of the leg.

But the Petticoat said:

"Your charms would have been vain without me, who made the most of you by hoisting myself up sufficiently to enable you to be seen, and served as a frame for your irresistible attractions. It's to my hypnotizing whiteness and to my troubling bell-ringing . . ."

"Which are my work," crackled the starch imprisoned in the fabric . . .

But the sofa laughed.

"What could you have done without me? What could the allure of your charms, less contestable for me because I have been able to observe their power many a time, better than anyone, have achieved without my aid? Am I not the supreme stage of the amorous hunt? Is it not between my arms, always obligingly open to illegitimate amours, that the irreparable fall is consummated? I am the furniture of adultery. The Bed only comes after me, never before. How many women would still be the forcibly faithful wife of a detested husband if they had not encountered, at the psychological moment—so fleeting and unique—in which the brain is deranged and the will softens, the mute elasticity of my cushions, to muffle the resonance of their fall?"

Suddenly, as harmonious and plaintive as the quavering vibration of a breaking harpstring, a voice murmured:

"I was the modesty of women, and the safeguard of husbands who knew that their honor was sufficiently padlocked in the prison of my batiste. All the enticements of stockings, capsizers of virtue, and petticoats, sowers of desires, ran piteously aground before the 'you shall go no further' of my unassailable citadel. The Sofa itself could do nothing against me. It required the complicity of the Bed to vanquish me. The Bed?—which is to say, the premeditated and resolute fall, the decision that never inhabits the flighty mind of women *the first time*.

"But one day a perversity arrives that cuts through my shield with a thrust of the scissors."

"Who are you, then, you who are lamenting?" enquired the Sofa, who was no longer laughing.

And the voice responded, as plaintive and melodious as the quavering vibration of a breaking harp-string:

"I am the soul of the closed Bloomers."

STAMMERINGS

IN the somber street, into which the sunlight scarcely slid through the high chimneys plumed with blue-tinted smoke;

In the narrow street rarely used as a short-cut by cabs, which did not know it;

In the tranquil street, into which not even policemen came in pairs to trouble the bleak silence with their rhythmic stride;

On the ribbonesque sidewalk of the somber, narrow and tranquil street;

In an obscure corner of the ribbonesque sidewalk, a little girl eight years old is sitting, her parted legs flat on the bitumen and her fists on her thin thighs.

With a limpid gaze, which not the slightest glimmer of curiosity comes to trouble, she follows the hand of a small boy ten years old, who, very red with a fiery gaze, is drawing in chalk on the sidewalk in the angle of her legs, shivering at the audacious obscenity, an enormous, erect, hirsute, monstrously accurate phallus, in the stammer of the sketch.

And while the sly boy watches the little girl's eyes hopefully, for the moist gleam that is shining in his own, the girl, without a crease in her lip or a single drop of blood more in her cheek, considers with a disinterested gaze that has KNOWN for a long time the enormous, erect, hirsute, phallus that the sly boy is drawing on the ribbonesque sidewalk of the narrow, somber and tranquil street.

THE TROUBLER OF MEN

SHE only left after putting herself under arms. And it is really her of whom one could say that she is armed to the teeth; for she had, by way of a dagger, a smile as sharp as a Malay krise, shining ferociously in its crimson scabbard.

She was armed from top to toe, from her shiny ankle-boot, which molded with its fine kidskin the audacious curve of her improbably tiny foot, to her coquettish Henri II hat, topped by a cascading ostrich plume, under which the blue gleam of her gaze sparkled.

And it was with a savantly scrupulous science, of Machiavellian study, that she proceeded, perhaps for hours, with the toilette of undergarments that she knew, pertinently, to be irresistible, when, with a grandiose regal air, she gave the alms of a barely-glimpsed coin to the begging eyes that watched out for her as she passed by.

She was a past master in the exquisite art of profiting from black stockings against the white backcloth of underskirts with edges trimmed with fine lace.

She knew the exact place where the garter of the bloomers ought to close, neither too low to allow the entire leg to be seen nor too high to render it disgraceful.

She studied for a long time, in her mirror, the effect that she was soon going to produce, and repeated her lesson in advance, in order to know, when she went out, where to grip her underskirt with an indifferent hand in order to allow the sight, without seeming to be aware of it, neither too much not too little, of what she had to show.

Once the lesson was thoroughly known, she departed, practicing instinctively the precept of Dandyism: "A dandy can put ten hours into his costume, but once it is on, he forgets it." And certainty, if the perverse person put ten hours into learning her role, she forgot so completely that it was only a role that she became, by dint of art, *naturally* ingenuous.

Along the sidewalks where the ostrich plume caused busy pedestrians to hasten their pace, or, on days of bright sunlight, via dusty avenues where her brightly-colored dress blossomed under the verdure of the trees as cheerful and fresh as a flower, she trotted, boldly tucked-up under the pretext of mud or dust, allowing the sight of her eternal black stockings, sculpturally enticing, outlined against the package of white petticoats, which left behind her a wake of iris and freshly-cut hay.

And, marching behind her, allured and magnetized by her leg, beardless schoolboys regaled themselves, and old men reinvigorated by the free spectacle rediscovered their vigor of twenty years in order to run for kilometers under the spell.

And an entire hungry pack galloped after her, astonished at first to be so numerous following the same trail, and then becoming anxious at always finding themselves as the same distance from one another, examining one another curiously on the sly, ashamed, in the end, of surprising the same gaze in one another's eyes, the same obsessive thought in pursuit of the same goal.

As she always went out at the same time, invariably following the same itinerary, it was almost always the same hypnotized individuals, young and old, that trotted behind her. At length they finished up knowing one another, and as they knew *why they were there*, it was with blushing faces that they hastened, without daring to break the silence with a word—not even the one that they all had on their lips, which they dared not pronounce.

Sometimes, in order to cast the same unforeseen disturbance in all their hearts, she interrupted her course abruptly, half-turned toward them, stopped, leaned forward, and slowly, enjoying their enjoyment, under their moist gazes, she pulled up her fine pink garter, *which had not fallen.*

They stood there, in shock, nailed to the spot and breathless; then, when she set off again, the charm broken, they resumed their interested stroll.

On certain days, in order to put her pack of adorers off the track, she amused herself by climbing to the top deck of a tram, revolutionizing as she went up the people on the platform, including the conductor, blasé as he was with regard to the quotidian spectacle.

And at the stops, as everywhere else, when the tram went past, men paused, noses in the air, agglutinated by that wave of white petticoats serving as a backcloth to the spellbinding black stockings, the stubborn memory of which haunted them when the vehicle had departed.

And every evening she went to sleep, blissfully, with a thin sly smile at the corners of her mouth, seeming to say like Titus of Roman memory: "I haven't wasted my day."

IN THE OMNIBUS

MISERABLE and distressing, on one of the once-blue banquettes strained with large patches of dirty grease, a woman standing out from the others by virtue of her vulgar ugliness, her complexion splashed with freckles and her pitifully common features.

Facing her, an improbably handsome young man, imperturbably disdainful, whose gaze declares plainly enough the scorn in which he holds the ambient banality.

And as SHE holds out her six sous in a red, bony hand, as bumpy and crumpled as an old glove, it is the aristocratic right hand of the *very handsome* man that offers itself first to pass the coins of the *very ugly* woman to the conductor.

Can it be that extreme Beauty and extreme Ugliness have an impalpable and invisible point of contact, unsuspected by the Mediocre, in which the fluid of SYMPATHY is exchanged electrically?

THE CHILD-SCARER

THE bizarre obstinacy that he put into only following women whose arms were embarrassed by children still in swaddling clothes—nurses with long crimson ribbons dangling to their ankles or young mothers strutting the recent joy of exhibiting the fruit of their legal fornications—had interested me to such a point that I started following the enigmatic follower.

Nothing enticed him in a bright stocking glimpsed beneath a frilly petticoat, nor a thin waist that caused the bulbous opulence of the bust to stand out, nor even the riotous undulations of an exaggerated rump stirring up a wake of iris and amber.

His strolling only latched on to the heels of nurses, and it seemed to be the white linen of good children that hypnotized his retinas.

And it seemed to me that all the babies, whose pale gazes were wandering over the shoulders of the women carrying them, interested by the bustle of the street and the multicolored shine of the shop windows, suddenly fixed a troubled gaze, then anxious and then fearful, upon the eyes of the stroller who was following the women without saying a word to them, under the incitement of I know not what motive. And suddenly, in spite of one nursemaid's "Who's a bad boy!" scolding that inexplicable change of humor, the babies, whom that shadow Fear was darkening the iris and casting darkness through the dilated pupil into the depths of gazes, burst into trident, convulsive, terrified sobs and abruptly threw themselves backwards in order *not to see.*

And when the child, having calmed down, hazarded a moist gaze once again at the mute and correct stroller who was still following, the same sudden explicable Fear convulsed his face and the spasm of the same sobs gripped his belly.

And among all the infants that he followed that day, I remarked that gaze, vague at first, retained thereafter, then that fearful vision, and then those somersaults, those sobs, that Terror!

And always, as the intrigued woman turned round, anxious and interrogative, she encountered the cold, dignified, impassive visage of the mysterious idler.

Suddenly, as a further baby was frightened by looking at him, an oblique mirror came unexpectedly to give me the solution to the problem.

Profiting from a moment when no one could see him, the man had abruptly contorted his features in a grimace of terrifying ugliness, in order to scare the child, the only one who would see it.

THE DAISY

ALONG the causeway, where the rain had stopped, along the causeway flowery with white calves, those daisies of the asphalt that the sun had caused suddenly to grow, reflected in the puddles, and flecking the lustrous surface of the paving stones with gold, SHE hastens, briskly, brazenly tucking up in her left hand the packet of her white petticoats and showing, with such immodesty that she could not doubt it, her slender ankle, where the stocking is not dishonored by any wrinkle, and her plump, cambered, concupiscible calf, and down below—up above—far away, beyond the garter whose buckle latches on to a sunbeam, a nacreous corner of her incomparable thigh, which is liberated today from the modesty of bloomers.

A few steps behind is a pale adolescent devouring with gluttonous eyes—a starveling who has not been invited for a long time to such a pantagruelesque banquet—that slender ankle and that conscupiscible calf, and that nacreous corner of an incomparable thigh.

Then, finally sated, he approaches her egotistically and murmurs, in order that others cannot feast their eyes after him: "Madame, one can see your legs . . ."

Imperiously serene and superb, without even deigning to turn her head, She lets fall from the height of her impassive indifference the monosyllables:

"I know."

THE DOG IS MAN'S FRIEND

FRATERNALLY, on the narrow sidewalk of the mute street, animated at rare intervals by the rapid footsteps of a passer-by, in front of the bottle-green little greengrocer's shop where stout choleriferous melons are swelling their gilded and sweet-smelling slices in vain, in the hope of hooking an enthusiast, a large Newfoundland dog is capering in concert with a child of four or five years, of whom he is the best and only comrade.

Suddenly, as the child had fallen into the gutter in the struggle and his squeals of joy responded to the resounding barking of the Newfoundland, alarmed by that fall, the father, convinced that the dog had knocked the child over, emerged abruptly from the shop.

And as the dog tried to bring the child back to the sidewalk, while the latter, still shaking with laughter, put both his arms around the huge hairy head, from which the enormous caressant tongue was dangling through the double row of formidable teeth, the father made the dog go back inside with a brutal kick, and chained him up.

And the child, seeing the father, barbaric and unjust because he had not seen anything but was inflicting a punishment anyway, chain his friend up at the entrance to the little bottle-green shop where the choleriferous melons were swelling their gilded and sweet-smelling slices in vain, started sobbing.

And without the thought occurring to him of protesting against the human injustice of being punished for a sin he had not committed, the dog, seeing his comrade desolate at seeing him tied up, feigned a happy expression, in order to console the child.

EGOTISMS

HER head is framed in the yellow lace of the white pillow, where her hair, uncurled for a long time, was tangled in disorder: in lace less yellow than her complexion, her former lily-white complexion, where all the wax seems to have run from the candles that will burn tomorrow to either side of the cadaver.

Through the mist of hair uncurled for a long time, her eyes, aureoled by the bistre of phthisis, dart a dark gaze at her lover—disinterested by that death, which is dragging on—whose egotistical amour has been gradually worn away by the angles of that thinness.

The strange fixity of her dark gaze, which is blazing in her dilated pupils, troubles the lover, who is prowling around the room, vaguely decked out in a mask of sympathy, to the extent of embarrassment.

With the clear sight of people who are about to die, she senses that the man has only ever loved the flesh in her, in her who had given him everything: heart, soul and body. And before that discovery of the final hour, a cry escapes her throat:

"The other . . . the one with whom you will replace me when I'm no more . . . do you know her?"

He protests, without conviction:

"Can you believe that, my darling? You will be my only amour."

"You're lying," she roars, between her teeth, which are already clicking with the spasms of her death-throes.

And after a silence that he dares not interrupt, she says, in an excited voice, whipped by commencing delirium:

"But I shall come back from *out there*; I shall come back during moonless nights to haunt your alcove and blow fear into the midst of your caresses. My stubborn Shade will strive to enervate the quiet lassitudes and sweet annihilations of the aftermaths of your amour . . ."

"I beg you, my adored," he hazards, "not to excite yourself so . . ."

"I don't want . . ." she bursts forth, "I don't want . . . no, I don't want you . . . to love another woman after me."

And as, leaning over her, he kissed her on the forehead in order to calm her excitement, a red flash striped the green sky of her iris; and with a supreme effort, drawing her lover's head toward her with her knotted arms, she bit him hard on the neck, and, with a clash of teeth whose force was multiplied a hundredfold by fever, she sliced through his carotid.

And while that banal lover, to whom she had given everything and whom she had adored until death, was dying; while a jet of blood sprang from the artery, turning the white pillow crimson on which her hair, uncurled for a long time, was tangled in disorder, she expired blissfully.

THE HUMBLE

IN the intimate studio as large as a box of chocolates, modestly hidden between two gigantic gardens of the Versaillesque Rue Monsieur, the large stove is purring and the November sunlight, anemic and icy, insinuates itself between the vast curtains.

The master is not there, and the paintings take advantage of it to chat among themselves.

On the massive easels, the grandiose proud portraits brace themselves in their gilded frames. They praise one another loudly for their vigorous colors and the Rembrantesque play of light with which the painter has been lavish. They know that they will be going to the next Exhibition and that the bourgeois will be dazzled by them. Some are coming back from Holland, or Munich, or even further away, and telling their neighbors about the ovations with which enthusiastic crowds saluted them out there. They take pride in the suffrage of juries who forbade them to die because they are the sons of the fay Inspiration. Spoiled by success, that rust of the great, they scarcely give the alms of a pitying glance to the Humble, as Valadon[1] calls them, to the exquisitely living still lifes, hidden in discreet corners as if in penitence, hung beneath disdainful drapes in the shadow of the massive easels where the great proud portraits brace themselves in their gilded frames.

On minuscule canvases that are not designated to the gaze by any gilded frame, chilly cats arch their backs, their eyes blinking and their paws drawn back, huddled in gray rapture, the little bright-burning stoves beside the heart-rending rags that are hanging from the sill of a melancholy window. Oh, the penetrating poetry of melancholy little windows whose dusty panes filter a Rembrandtesque daylight! Oh, the gaiety that render thoughtful the minuscule bright-burning gray stoves, the crackling purr of which accompanies the satisfied purr of the chilly cats which arch their backs, their eyes blinking and their paws drawn back, huddled beneath the real little stoves, rapturously gray.

And during the absence of the Master, I have left the vanities of the great portraits, which are His glory, to glorify one another, and I surprise myself listening to the chatter of the Humble, which are his joy, and which are a corner of his soul.

---

1 The model-turned-painter Suzanne Valadon (1865-1938), who eventually made her reputation with bold nude studies; she was at the very beginning of that second career when the present collection was published, mostly drawing things that she saw around her.

DEDUCTION

If you are not false, oh are you true?
—Tristan Corbière[1]

WHEN I asked him for the secret of the arrogant and imperturbable indifference with which he was armored in regard to women—an indifference of which they tried to soften the impertinence by explaining it by a vice he did not have, although he was so sovereignly scornful of that great whore Public Opinion that he almost took pride in being accused of it—Kerbihan replied:

"The secret is simple, my dear friend, and I consent to dispossess myself of it in your favor.

"Every woman, her beauty as well as her finesse, her charms as well as her flair and her sphinxism—in brief, her entire psychic personality as well as her physical person—is merely a convention. The power that the female preserves over almost all males is the logical

1 Tristan Corbière (1845-1875), born, like Léo Trézenik, in Brittany, was one of the *Poètes maudits* lauded in Paul Verlaine's classic 1884 anthology.

consequence and the inevitable result of the illusion that she provides for them. The woman—I mean the woman of their imagination, the woman that they would like, the mirage, the illusion, the virtuality by which they are duped—is all accessories. She would not exist if she were only herself. Everything that she seems to be is a creation of our desires, an optical effect to which the gaze becomes accustomed and eventually ends up believing to be a reality. At first one has seen her as one would have liked her to be; then, thanks to the marvelous presentiment that she has of our needs, she composes herself as one would like her to be—which is to say, all curves and perfumes here, all sentiments and sensations there, wholly artificial. Her mind is an echo of ours, her vocabulary the produce of that education of a well-taught parrot that the man has given her.

"Now, if it is true that every female psyche is the creation of men, it is no less indubitable that she owes her physical charms to the interested munificence of men. In other words, a woman is not beautiful in herself, she is only beautiful because men believe her to be.

"She has been called a necessary evil; that is only half true. She is an evil, but one that is only necessary for the weak. The healthy and the strong willingly liberate themselves from the need which a woman is the means of satisfying, from which she alone profits, and the slaking of which, under whatever sonorous name it is disguised, is a sullying.

"That being posited, my means, finally to arrive at it, of mocking the attraction of woman, whenever I am on the point of submitting to it, is this:

"When I am in the presence of a woman, when she is cackling, surrounded by an attentive court, in the moist languidness of a brightly illuminated drawing room, or fluttering her rump at the level of Lutecian displays, her skirt tucked up as far as the ankle, I disarm her in a second, I dissolve the mirage, I blow away the iridescent illusion . . ."

"In what fashion?" I interrupted, in order to bring him back to his famous means.

"I undress her instantly in thought; I make an abstraction of the dress whose magnetized silk and audacious and boastful bulges only cover a void; I remove the corset that shores up and sustains, which repels, displaces, replaces and harmonizes; my pitiless eye drills through the underclothes, the whiteness of which refreshes and the malines embalms;

"And I no longer have anything before me but the ridiculous spectacle of a grotesque nudity, flaccid and overflowing, striped with red blotches and stitched with streaks, damp and acrid-smelling, prancing on excessively short legs and making graces 'with the assent of dangling breasts';

"And as it is pointless to manifest a hilarity that would remain inexplicable to the person provoking it, I keep quiet, and only permit myself a smile easily mistaken for a sign of approval and a polite acquiescence to the musky vulvarities and inept simperings of the charming parrot, who cannot imagine the extent to which her chirping is amusing when it is heard without her plumage.

"And that's the whole of my secret."

41

THE CANINE TRINKET

HEAD down, with an indefinable expression of bitterness in the upward gaze with which it seems to be begging the passer-by, it trots on the heels of its mistress, the pitiful barbet shorn "like a lion."

Its denuded tail, which terminates in a ridiculous black pompom, is curled between its legs, also shorn, with the exception of a tuft of curly hair that emphasizes, three centimeters from the claws, the diaphanousness of its thin limbs, shivering with shame rather than cold.

Its head brushes the sidewalk, as if crushed by the weight of the ridiculous blue ribbon that has been knotted in a rosette on its cranium, and its caricaturish pseudoleonine mane, which clashes with the marbled nudity of its black pelt, does what it can to hide the little blue collar on which a minuscule bell of shiny copper tinkles dolorously in its ears.

It senses that it has the absurdly pretty appearance of an astrakhan pooch descended from its display-shelf, and it makes itself very small along the boutiques, the poor ashamed dog that goes head down, with an indefinable expression of bitterness in the upward gaze with which it seems to be begging the passer-by.

Suddenly, at the corner of a populous street, a bulldog that is passing by at a gallop, improbably dirty, its tail rigid and its proud head striped by an enormous wrinkle that further accentuates the insolence of its gaze, stops momentarily before it.

And as the pitiful mock-lion tries to dissimulate its shame in the dark corner of an awning, the bulldog looks it up and down scornfully. And, pretending to mistake it for an absurdly pretty astrakhan pooch descended from its display-shelf. It turns its head slowly, in which the enormous wrinkle that stripes its forehead becomes even more pronounced; then, lifting its leg disdainfully, it pisses on it.

THE OMNIBUS DRIVER

IT was a fine coachman's mug; rutilant, crimson, improbably glabrous, his face was a dazzling block of onyx striped with pink and veined with azure arabesques that entangled their mesh all around the nose, and enormous amethyst crammed with vermilion raspberries growing there as if in soil. His broad mouth, with lips as thin as a sword-cut, was hollowed out in the left corner by a minuscule fissure from which dangled, at a fixed angle, a little short-stemmed pipe, black half-way to the bowl, which he was smoking expertly in little puffs, a connoisseur emeritus knowing the profound art of making that ephemeron Pleasure last. To either side of the nose shone two bright eyes, ultramarine-ash-gray in color, whose gaze, charged with a profound malice, had astonishing fulgurations.

I observed in that physiognomy certain originalities of detail that struck me. The singular phosphorescence that shone in his eyes had a very particular glare, and the half-smile that creased the corner of his lip was too extra-common for the brain that was its point of departure to be made of vulgar substance.

Involuntarily, gripped again by that customary obsession, the mania of observation, I set about examining him attentively.

"Don't think," he said to me suddenly, without transition, as if he had penetrated my thought and wanted to give me the solution of a problem that was haunting me, "that our métier is only brutalizing. Some of us—rare, it's necessary to admit—are able, without descending from their seat, to forge very distinguished distractions. Thus I, such as you see me," he affirmed, accentuating slightly the crease that cut the corner of his lip, "am refined, and it is partly in order to savor and to enable the savoring of emotions similar to mine."

"Give me the key to this puzzle," I said to him as we emerged, at the nonchalant petty trot of his three horses, at the summit of the Rue Notre-Dame-de-Lorette.

"You can easily find it on your own." And he enveloped his percherons with a broad stroke of the whip, the unexpected sharp bite of which awoke them from their torpor and launched them, backs braced, manes in the wind and heads high, along the steep slope that leads to the Place Saint-Georges. The enormous vehicle, lifted up like a mere cab by its vigorous team, bounded over the pavement with a deafening sound of mirrors cascading in their frames and maddened wheels tearing, with their iron armor the brutally-scraped edge of the sidewalk.

Frightened, the few women on the top deck fell silent, their eyes closed and their spines shivering fearfully against the back of the banquette. Wan shopkeepers emerged from their shops in haste considered with a hint of interest the stout omnibus that was tumbling vertiginously down the steep street.

"The coachman must be drunk," their big round eyes seemed to say, magnified by amazement, "to come down this dangerous street at that speed."

A few prudent fathers of families tried to make my friend understand the imprudence of that frantic trot. He did not even respond. Strangely enough, the abruptly-whipped air that cut off the respiration did not produce any of its habitual intoxication on him. He remained cold, smiling imperceptibly. It was not the exquisite sensation of a void in the lungs produced by rapid velocity that he was seeking.

What, then?

Suddenly, at the corner of the Place Saint-Georges, the vehicle lurched; its speed was such that the two wheels on the left quit the ground momentarily. Everyone, without exception, instantaneously had the sensation that the tilting omnibus was about to be projected to a nearby shop. An immense cry of terror sprang up everywhere; but the vehicle had already found its center of gravity again.

"This is my triumph," said the coachman in a low voice. "I calculated my speed exactly to produce the result that you've just observed, but between us, I don't think I've ever succeeded as well as today; I feel understood."

We had arrived in the Rue Châteaudun.

"Well," he said to me, "you can see that there are still good moments in our métier."

NEWS ITEM

WITH the taut cord at the end of her elongated arm that was gently pulling a little dog, the old woman is trotting hurriedly, tapping the edge of the sidewalk with her walking-stick.

The old woman is blind and the dog is deaf.

For three years they have united their miseries, and are identified with one another to the point that they are now only a single individual, of whom the old woman is the hearing and the dog the vision; the old woman sees via the dog's gaze and the dog hears by means of the of woman's ears. In the cord that links them together, I know not what electric frissons pass, which put the two souls in communication and unify their sensations so well that they trot through the mazy streets of the city with the same security as if the old woman could see and the dog could hear.

One day, at the corner of a street, the little dog descended from the sidewalk momentarily and squatted in the gutter. The blind woman understood and stopped. Suddenly, a heavy vehicle came up behind them, which did not see the little dog, and as the dog was deaf and the electric frissons that came from the old woman's hearing were no longer passing along the slackened cord, the dog did not hear the vehicle, which broke its back.

The old woman's gaze was extinguished.

The old woman had become blind again.

CHARITY

FLORID in a bright dress on which chimerical pink birds flew over a mysterious azure background, SHE illuminated with a bright patch the monotonous rank of bimanes whose shoulders collided at every jolt of the heavy vehicle all along the trellised banquette of the top deck. Her Lilliputian feet, lightly posed one atop the other, uncovered the corner of a cerulean stocking embroidered with golden arabesques when the wind of the passage caused the flap of her bright dress, on which chimerical pink birds were flying over a mysterious azure background, to undulate gently.

At the bus stop, timid and as if ashamed of his worn but stainless jacket, the shiny thread of which was transparent, a poor wretch was stammering, very close to the vehicle, the offer of red pencils destined to dissimulate the thin and diaphanous hand extended to the charity of passers-by.

And as his gaze, in which a desperate gleamed of desire flashed, reposed for a second on the settled flap of the bright dress that illuminated with a bright patch

49

the monotony of the top deck, SHE had the intuition of alms so regal that she alone could give them, and in order momentarily to gild that misery with the reflection of the opulence of her beauty, she suddenly lifted up the flap of her bright dress, under the pretext of crossing her legs, granting to the gaze of that indigent of all joys, that victim of all hungers, the unexpected license to caress his gaze, bewildered by such a marvelous gift, the sculptural line of her cerulean stocking embroidered with golden arabesques.

And the wretch had, in consequence, a sunlit soul; more so, surely, than if a gold coin had fallen unexpectedly into his hat.

And in a low voice, which gratitude cause to tremble, he murmured:

"God will render it to you, my good lady!"

TENDERNESS

ALONG the steep slope, a huge percheron, breathless and straining in the shafts, is clinging to the heavy cart; its robust neck, where its white mane is cascading, is wrinkling under the effort; its respiration is wheezing and fuming through its palpitating nostrils, and, its flanks gripped by fatigue and stabbed by anguish, it is moaning, gasping and lamenting.

The horse has stopped, half-fainting, but the brutal carter has enveloped it abruptly with the sting of his whip, which bites and tears, and the valiant animal persists, clinging to the heavy cart, its robust neck wrinkling in the effort.

The load is too great and the slope too steep; the horse strives in vain, breathless between the shafts.

And without any intervention of the passers-by, whose egotism is disinterested in that unequal struggle, the carter strikes, strikes and strikes the poor beast, which flattens its ears and shakes its head, as if it wanted to make the brute—who is the master of that intelligence by virtue of the law of the strongest—understand the impossibility of going any further.

And suddenly, in a supreme effort to which it is incited and constrained by a new and more agonizing bite of the pitiless whip, the horse loses its equilibrium and, scraping the pavement noisily with its four iron shoes, collapses on the ground with a gasp of pain.

When the horse regains its feet, painfully and tremulously, the carter, his eyes moist and his expression anxious, examines the beast's knees at length, and gently, maternally, with "Oh my Gods" that move the idlers to pity, he wipes them with his blouse in order to make sure that the mud is not dissimulating any wound.

Because that would prevent him from selling it later.

CHILD'S PLAY

IN the crushing torpor of a somnolent evening, at the high window wide open over the park, where the leafy plane-trees are agitating the languid fan of their branches gently, with the soft rhythm of a caress, two children are leaning on their elbows, their gazes lost in a dreamy boredom, staring without seeing at the great rubescent sun setting in the distance, its last oblique rays drilling through the thick tangle of leafy boughs and powdering the flavescent hair of the two children with gold dust.

"Make me butterflies," the little sister begs, suddenly, already disinterested in the illusion of dolls.

And as the brother does not reply, and, his eyes staring, he refuses to extract himself from his vague reverie, the mysterious and troubling reverie of children that transports them to distant lands forgotten, alas, by those who have lived too long, she persists, with a pretty blue imploring gaze:

"I'll catch the flies for you."

And with her slender and diaphanous hand, where the azure network of veins runs beneath the transparency of delicate skin, she catches a fly that is confidently cleaning itself on the sunlit edge of the high window.

By condescension, more to rid himself of an insistence who obstinacy he foresees, the brother briskly decapitates the fly with an expert fingernail into a piece of paper, folded in two, which his sister presents to him. Then, slipping the whole between the pages of a stout missal florid with naïve illuminations, he leans on the cover momentarily with both hands.

In the missal there is a little moist click.

And when they reopen it and unstick the two leaves of blank paper, the two children utter cries of admiration.

The head of the little fly had burst under the pressure; the gray splashes of the brain, the pink spurts of blood from the abruptly severed arteries, and the dots of the thousand scattered eyes of the fly traced a fantastic silhouette in the center of the sheet, with colors harmoniously melted and curiously jagged contours displayed on the sides and bizarrely elongated in the middle, the design of which evidently evoked, in the infantile imagination, the image of a multicolored and fantastic butterfly.

And the little sister, enthused, clapped her hands and cried, in her shrill little girlish voice:

"Again! Again!"

MARDI GRAS

MUTE and grave, very small and thin, he, scarcely six years old, very proud of being "aristocratic," with his leg bent, his back braced, his right hand in the gap of his waistcoat, from which the starched frills of the ruff emerge, the left hand clutching against his breast with a sort of respect a tricorn hat with a golden rim; she, dressed as a milkmaid, her little hands in the pockets of her minuscule white apron; their faces illuminated by joy, they are going along, tapping the sidewalk with their little varnished shoes.

They are trotting under the eyes, moist with joy, of the papa, the mama and the big sister, who are following, with blissful smiles on their lips, looking out for sudden expansions on the part of passers-by, and who turn round, delighted when an admiring exclamation bursts forth: "Aren't they pretty, those children!" or disappointed when they pass an indifferent philosopher whom such masquerades leave cold; but they retain, fixed at the corners of the lips, the half-closed smile that will blossom triumphantly a hundred paces further on, polite thanks addressed to the worthy people—parents themselves!—who stop to stroke with their hand the crimson cheeks of the little play-actors.

In the meantime, Monsieur gives Madame, while Mademoiselle yawns while watching men dressed as women and women dressed as men pass by, in order to signify her opinion of the death of the Paris carnival.

"In Nice, you see, everyone is masked, Mardi Gras is obliged to exist. Why is everyone masked? It's quite simple: because of the confetti."

"The confetti?"

"The confetti," explains Monsieur, who has traveled, "are little balls of plaster as big as peas, which are thrown in the face in handfuls. As that's horribly nasty, everyone is masked in order to protect them. It's no more complicated than that."

"That's very ingenious."

And the children are still trotting, lost in the crowd on the boulevards, emerged "to see the masks." They stretch themselves in vain behind that hedge of backs, desolate at passing unperceived, while the parents strive to fray a passage for them with thrusts of the elbows and shoulders. Sometimes Madame utters a little cry and Mademoiselle exclaims: "Imbecile!" It's a foot that has been trampled in the confusion or a kiss that resounds, planted in flight on the back of the neck, while bright laughter flows from the horrible painted mask of the "imbecile," suddenly withdrawn into the crowd.

They are going to dinner with the grandmother, on a tranquil street where one can breathe a little. Two pierrots pass by, absurdly gray and bumping into the wall in turn. Further on, a Lois XIII seigneur in a frilly doublet is making haste, his left hand proudly leaning on a long rapier, which makes a metallic sound against his thin calves, clad in ocher hose.

In the grandmother's house the place of honor is given to "Monsieur le Marquis," who ends up taking his title seriously, by virtue of hearing it repeated; so he refuses energetically to allow his napkin to be tied around his neck, as it was yesterday. He wants to put it in his lap, "like little father." That is why, in the second course, he soils his beautiful silk waistcoat with grease, and drops an entire spoonful of little peas into the frilly shirt. Consequence: a maternal slap.

Grandmama is annoyed: "Hitting a child! On a day like this!"

"That's my business," replies the mother, slightly bitterly.

In brief, they separate in a very bad mood and they leave in order to put Monsieur le Marquis to bed, along with the poor little milkmaid, who has stuffed herself so much with chocolate cream that she throws up in the carriage all over her lovely white apron and her pretty little red dress.

THE ART OF BREAKING UP

"LISTEN to this, Kerbihan," said Charles, suddenly, absorbed until then in reading *Gil Blas*. "The man who compiles a good manual of the art of breaking up will render a greater service to humanity, especially to men, than the inventor of railways."

"To whom does that aphorism belong?" enquired Kerbihan, woken up by the whimsy.

"A certain Maufrigneuse, who is offering, in an article, some advice to a friend desirous of breaking up with an obsolete mistress."

"What advice?"

"Oh, nothing much: poisoning her, taking the plunge, having oneself caught *in flagrangte delicto* by the husband, becoming a priest, blowing one's brains out, etc. Nothing new, as you can see."

"Banalities," sniggered Kerbihan. "There's only one means of breaking up, one alone, that I had long desired to formulate in a concise manual under the title *The Art of Breaking Up*, in order to provide a companion to my *Art of Making Oneself Loved.*[1] But I feared that Monsieur Paul Ginisty, who is a fine critic, was reserving for the poor *Art of Breaking Up* the discouraging mockery with which he greeted *The Art of Making Oneself Loved,* and I've broken my pen."

"That's all right," protested Léon Sylvain, "the reason you're pretexting for keeping quiet isn't peremptory, and we'll believe in your means when *The Art of Breaking Up* appears."

"It will never appear. What's the point? Who would understand it? And how many would put it into practice? And yet, that means exists," Kerbihan affirmed. "It's unique, and it would be an admirable subject of psychic and analytic study. As my idleness on the one hand and my philosophical nihilism on the other will prevent me from writing that study, it would please me to see it developed by some authorized pen. That's why I'm going to formulate it for you in a few words, with the hope that a skillful one might be able to profit from it.

"First of all, let's establish our characters.

"She is still in love, he isn't. She doesn't want to quit him for the sole reason that she loves him. There's no need to search for another. And in a moment of expansion, one day when he is testing the ground, and he has asked, between two kisses, what she would do if he quit her, she has responded in a slightly veiled voice that she would kill herself. And he has seen the blue of her retina darken at that question.

---

1 Trézenik had, in fact, published a book entitled *L'Art de se faire aimer* [The Art of Making Oneself Loved] in 1883. Kerbihan is the name of a seaside resort in his native Brittany.

"As, on the other hand, he knows that she is a woman ready for anything, he understands that it isn't a pose, and that she would do it. Let's admit, if you wish, that he fears, either because of the scandal or because of the ridicule that the death in question would cause to rebound on him. What is he to do?

"What is the obstacle to the rupture here? The love that she has for him. So, it's that love that it's necessary to kill

"First of all, how did he make himself loved?

"He played for a month the comedy of amour, exquisitely, as a refined virtuoso. He has magnetized her with his clear and penetrating gaze in which the artificial flame burned that he alone ignited, but in which she believed. He has dazzled her with the fireworks of his mind, disseminating sparkling and multicolored paradoxes. He has edified a pedestal on to which he has climbed, a false figure that her illusion, created by his art, has dressed splendidly.

"He has only allowed himself to be seen through a prism speckled with sparks that his deceptive hand has placed before her eyes. He causes to shine before her, eternally, the fake gems that she has mistaken for diamonds. He has been able to play his role of idol so well that at present she still sees him on his throne, in all the fulgurance of his glory and all his godlike power.

"Well, in order to break up, the god quite simply descends to the human again.

"He is going to take away, bit by bit, all the scintillating radiance with which he has been pleased thus far to aureole his brow; he is going to blow away, one by one, all the illusions of the poor abused woman. He is finally going to take off his mask.

"His entire tactic, now that he wants to break up, consists of doing the opposite of what he attempted in order to make himself loved. He is going to play 'who loses wins.' He is going to kill the amorous effect by destroying, one by one, its causes.

"You all know Stendhal's theory of crystallization. Now, in the present case, the crystallization has not operated spontaneously and instinctively; he is the one who has directed it; he is the only author responsible for it. Well, now he is going to break, one after another, all the little crystals that have accumulated slowly.

"He has composed a visage, confected a role, put on a disguise. He is going to contract his muscles in a contrary direction and his smile will become a grimace. He is going to cry out in all his words, all his actions and all his silences that 'what I said yesterday was a lesson learned by heart; it was false, my dear, I'm an impostor of amour.'

"He is going to throw that carnival costume into the nettles, quit his sparkling azure doublet dappled with gold, unhook his rapier and show beneath that borrowed fancy dress the sordidness of his true garments, the ones that are really his. He is going to employ all his cares putting in relief what he previously kept carefully hidden, physical imperfections as well as moral flaws. In a word, he is going to demolish, piece by piece, the figure that he put all his art into building.

"That's the beginning.

"Many women will be satisfied with less, and will break up of their own accord one fine morning when they wake up with the disillusioned cry on their lips, risen from the heart: 'So he's *a man like all the rest!* My God, how was I able to deceive myself to this degree?' without thinking that it was him who, wanting her to be 'deceived to that degree,' and who—because he still wants that—is undeceiving her at the hour marked by his will.

"You will glimpse the theory sufficiently to foresee that with certain more tenacious women it will be necessary to go as far as overtly unjust reproaches, provocative of torrential tears. In that case, unexpected departures will do well, accompanied by Parthian shots of a cold cruelty, skirting vulgarity, of this sort: 'That's great! Here comes the rain. I'll come back when you're dry.'

"A month of that regime is sufficient to demolish the most solid amour. In general, though, it isn't necessary to go that far. Gradual disillusionment, carefully crafted and complete, will suffice. Of her own accord, the crumbled, disorganized, annihilated woman will request an amiable separation. And you will have attained your goal: a definitive, irrevocable rupture, obtained artistically and without the slightest shock.

"I defy any woman, no matter how infatuated, to resist that means."

ODORLESS PHILOSOPHY

NEAR the bus stop where the calm dappled grays are getting bored, gazing at the pavement, their necks hanging down, their long tangled manes almost reaching the ground; not far from the old church where crouching beggars are mewling under the ogival porch, the minuscule once-yellow fir-wood cabin, the unnamable utilitarian cabin, opens its hospitable door, the door on which Madame the Attendant is leaning, waiting for clients.

As her clientele consists almost entirely of "messieurs priests" who are coming to say their morning masses or, in the evening, to confess the blissful devotees, she has taken on a mystically clerical air that suits her face, wrinkled like an old apple and slashed by a toothless mouth, by a broad black gap that has the form of an accolade. She has the hands, browned as much by amassed dirt as tanned by the years, of aged attendants of the sick.

The minuscule once-yellow fir-wood cabin, the unnamable utilitarian cabin, as big at the most as a Norman wardrobe, is divided into six narrow cupboards into which, silently and discreetly, messieurs the priests who are coming to say their morning masses or, in the evening, to confess the blissful devotees, are engulfed.

Only five doors open from time to time, for Madame the Attendant has reserved the sixth cupboard.

It is there that she cooks, between two bibs, on the seat, which dissimulates a movable table.

Twice a day, as she cannot quit the little house of which she is the guardian, she does her cooking in her cupboard, which reeks of fried onions: an honest aroma that evokes the idea of the dark and smoky back rooms where petty grocers prepare meals. Stoical and philosophical, she opens the doors between two mouthfuls, invites a client to penetrate into those ephemeral homes, rinses a porcelain with her hasty and habituated hand, and returns to her hole to supervise the onions frying on her little stove, alongside a diarrhoetic and cataractant "monsieur priest."

Near the bus stop where the calm dappled grays are getting bored, the minuscule once-yellow fir-wood cabin, the unnamable utilitarian cabin, opens its hospitable door, the door on which Madame the Attendant is leaning, waiting for clients.

SIGNS

HAVE you noticed how much respect and terror Monsieur Public has for signs that impertinently order him or forbid him suddenly to do something against his will or his whim?

A large octavo would scarcely suffice to narrate the mute loquacity of signs hanging on the wall that mock or slyly chide the discomfiture of Monsieur Public, on whom they play tricks as they please.

And it would require a poem in twelve thousand alexandrines to sing the resigned inconveniences of Monsieur Public, who subscribes, without even thinking about arguing, to the puerile demands of troublesome administrations.

NO SMOKING, trumpets some placard at the back of a tram station, where the smelly dirt of the employees' caps, the carbon oxide of the stove and the fetid emanations of breath fuse into a unique but violent stink.

And Monsieur Public, who has just come in, chewing a pleasantly scented London with a satisfied expression, although half-stunned by that unison of howling odors, precipitately throws his cigar away.

As if, through the placidity of the poster, the fading ink of which is beginning no longer to cut through the pissy velum, he had seemed to see the wide eyes of an alguazil ablaze, his spiky moustache bristling.

Sometimes signs draw in their claws. They take on soothing tones, softened expressions and caressant attitudes. *You are requested not to smoke.* And, less hasty before the politeness of that invitation, almost tempted to take off his hat, Monsieur Public serenely draws a few final puffs from his pleasantly scented London, which surround him with a possible atmosphere and give him time to habituate his lungs to the ambient stink that combines, by fusing them, the smelly dirt of the employees' caps, the carbon oxide of the stove and the fetid emanations of breath.

But whether they are polite or impertinent, Monsieur Public has the respect and terror of signs whose prohibition or invitation abruptly cuts across his will or his whim.

SUNDAY

THE stupid day *par excellence.*

So it is the one that correct people have chosen to amuse themselves. They have even created, for their personal use, the expression "to put on one's Sunday best."

And they go along the boulevards, too narrow for their crowd, arm in arm, husbands in long black frock-coats and women in silk dresses sparkling in the spring sunlight or dull beneath gray winter skies.

Early in the morning Monsieur has trimmed his beard, of which he has made a present to Madame in a fit of gallantry. Madame has brought out of the drawer her heavy white skirt, which she only wears on Sundays, and a bonnet that languishes all week at the back of the cupboard on its wooden peg.

"What if we have breakfast at the restaurant?" Madame suggests

"Good idea!"

And they go to poison themselves for thirty sous apiece—it's necessary to make economies—in some dingy guinguette in the neighborhood. At dessert, the traditional question is asked;

"What shall we do today?"

In summer, the Buttes-Chaumont and the Botanical Gardens extend their invitations. But in winter, when it is dry and the cold is biting, setting Monsieur's nose ruddily ablaze and turning Madame's ordinary pale complexion carmine under her veil . . .

"What if we were to go to the Musée de Cluny?"

For the Louvre and the Luxembourg either say nothing to them, or too much; Madame claims that those huge and cynical statues are indecent, which show . . . what Madame Dupré does not dare reveal even to her husband.

It is true that it might not take much for her to show them.

Cluny tempts them, with its old scrap metal, of which the couple understand nothing, but which permit Monsieur Dupré to give his wife a little imaginary history lecture here and here. And then, is there not the famous chastity belt, which one wants to see without admitting it, and which one inspects curiously from the corner of the eye, slyly, while pretending to ecstasize over our ancestors' enormous suits of armor.

"What fine fellows, eh, my friend, the men who could put on a suit in that Elboeuf!"

At the Arts et Métiers, two great attractions.

One can see, reflected in a mirror, people passing in the street, without suspecting that in a quarter of an hour, those passing by will be there, in the same place, watching those who are now here, passing by, and looking at them.

Then, downstairs, in the great elliptical hall, it is a "very amusing" tradition to exchange, in whispers, at opposite ends of the ellipse, enormous pleasantries, which can be heard in spite of the distance.

"A curious optical phenomenon," Monsieur observes.

Finally, four o'clock chimes. The Arts et Métiers closes and the lackeys drive the human flock before them, who will return in a week in order to reward themselves, before the same things, with the same dominical bewilderment.

"May I offer you a vermouth?" Monsieur says graciously to Madame; and they go to sit, in order to "watch the world going by" on the terrace of a little café, in which to postpone the necessity of going home to dinner.

As they are exhausted, they take the omnibus. But as everyone is in the same condition, they mark time for two hours, with a little piece of numbered cardboard in hand, outside the ticket office, crammed with people waiting. Madame envelops herself in vain in her wrap lined with rabbit-fur, and in vain Monsieur blows on his fingers and stamps his feet on the sidewalk; the north wind bites pitilessly, and they go home frozen. The fire isn't lit in the dining room, dinner isn't ready; the maid has gone out herself "to see a cousin who lives in Passy."

"Are you hungry?" says Madame.

"In truth, no," says Monsieur. "I'm tired. Shall we go to bed?"

And they go to sleep, harassed but content. They have enjoyed themselves.

THE GOOD GOD

ONE morning, God, who had been somnolent for billions and billions of years in damnable idleness, woke up with a very natural question on his lips:

"Where am I?"

"But I'm nowhere, since nothing but me exists.

"I exist without being anywhere; I exist in nothing; I'm nowhere, and yet I AM.

"Bizarre!

"But if that's an odd situation, on the one hand, it's intolerable on the other. And more than one sinister joker won't fail to abuse my position by declaring *urbi et orbi*—there isn't yet any *urbi* or any *orbi*, but it makes no difference—that I have no domicile, that I'm in a state of vagabondage. Perhaps they'll go as far as claiming that I can't exist in those conditions.

"It's definitely necessary for me to have a 'home,' as the English say—but no anachronisms!"

So, HE created the World—from nothing, naturally, since nothing existed. HE simply said: "Let the World be," and the World was.

Funnily enough, that hadn't cost him any fatigue, since he had only had to wish to do it. However, that wish took seven days—seven periods, if you prefer, it's necessary to satisfy everyone—to execute, during which God sat on a cloud blissfully being amazed by his work, the curvature of which he found astonishing; on the seventh HE rested

So, there was the world created, with its infinite multitude of heavenly bodies rolling in the immensity; but all of that—stars and nebulae, planets and moons—was only done, the gracious Fénelon informs us, by making use of Jabloskoff[1] during the night on the earth, that grain of sand lost in a corner of the ether, because, by day, God had installed a special luminary, which he called the sun.

One morning, when HE was wandering in his immense domicile in order to judge the excellent distribution of the rooms, the Creator arrived by chance on the abovementioned grain of sand, which he found quite deserted; and in order to populate it, and at the same time to make a puppet with which to distract himself, he created Man.

As he was in a generous mood, he gave him a magnificent orchard, which he planted with all sorts of fruit trees, but as he was also in a playful mood he placed a superb apple tree in the very center, saying to the Man:

---

1 The reference is to the "Yablochkov candle," a type of electric arc lamp invented in 1876, first demonstrated in the Avenue de l'Opéra during the Paris Exhibition of that year.

"You know, I forbid you to eat the fruits of this tree; you would know everything, good and evil, as well as I do, and that would irritate me."

The Man, still naïve—he was so new—did not think of making the remark that it would have been simpler not to put the tree there with the others, the number of which was already sufficient.

It is true to say, in order to excuse the Man, that God already knew what would happen, since the future had no secrets from him. The proof is that, in order to help him to disobey, God gave him a companion, a Woman.

Having done that. God reasoned as follows:

"So, there's man created; I've ordered him not to eat an apple from the famous tree, but I know very well that he's going to eat one, precisely because I've forbidden him to do it. Naturally, I'll punish him for his disobedience, and for that I'll expel him with his woman from the garden I gave him, and what's more, I'll punish all his descendants, who aren't guilty of the fault of the first humans; I'll punish them because I'm JUST.

"On the other hand, as I'm GOOD, I'll save them. I'll send them my son, who will be born of a virgin by . . . the operation of the Holy Spirit, and who will die in order to redeem them from a sin they won't have committed: that just individual, dying for the guilty who aren't, seems to me to be a sufficient reparation."

The Serpent, who happened to be passing, hissed: "But it would be much simpler not to constrain the

Man to disobey, in order to avoid the trouble of punishing him in his descendants, who will never understand what they have to do with it."

God replied to it:

"Logic hasn't been invented yet; you're in advance of the centuries to come, my lad, and humans will take a long time to see that I've been making fun of them."

MY CANE

ODD! But let's not anticipate.

The day when I bought it, the ribbon of sky unfurling over the Boul'Mich was an immaculate cobalt blue; one might have thought it the unknotted faille belt of a first communicant. The sun, which was shining from directly overhead, was cooking the craniums of the strollers, who were apoplectic beneath their top hats, while their boot-heels were almost sinking into the softened bitumen that was undulating under their soles.

The sun was heating there as conscientiously as if it had been paid by the beer-sellers of the Latin quarter. Thirst was ardent in all pharynxes, desiccated to such a degree by the more-than-equatorial temperature that silence gradually fell in all the groups. Bleak and languid, their blinking eyes half-closed because of the reflection of the sidewalk, the boulevardiers were strung out in bands on the terraces of the cafés, quaffing silently, while mopping their brows, the warm beer that did not slake their thirst.

Old Père Salomon, who has died since, alas—everything passes—was going up the boulevard, his eternal packet of canes under his arm. Level with the Source he stopped, his ferrety little gray eyes peering at the drinkers one after another.

"Not even one," he mumbled, "to pay for a bock."

And as I went past him: "A pretty cane, for five francs; that's nothing, it's an opportunity . . . and a bock into the bargain."

"Twenty sous."

"Here, take it."

I stood there, stupefied by the facility with which he let me have it, contrary to his habit, at the proposed price. I even remarked that he had a certain gratitude to me for ridding him of it.

During the discussion, the sky had darkened abruptly; the blue ribbon had turned black; large gray clouds were running above the chimneys, whipped up by a sudden wind; then, abruptly, a storm burst. The cane, which attracted the rain, made me think; I thought vaguely, as if involuntarily, of the hazel wands that sorcerers use to find subterranean springs.

This one was honest wood; it was the most vulgar of sticks, red mahogany, smooth, without a pommel. Nothing revealed to me, at first sight, the profound perversity of which I was subsequently to be the pitiful victim.

Hostilities commenced as soon as the next day. At the moment of going out it was impossible to put my hand on it. I was certain, however, of having deposited it, when I came in, on its own, in the corner of the fireplace beside the armchair. After an hour of vain, angry, obstinate searching I discovered it, fallen along the plinth, almost invisible in the angle of the parquet.

From then on, between the two of us, there was a strange struggle, in which I invariably came off worse. On days when the needle of the barometer was immutable stationed on "very dry" I spent hours looking for it. It did no good to put it in evidence the previous night on a chair beside my hat, next to the door. I found it in impossible retreats, under the caret, where it insinuated itself by I know not what artifice, behind the furniture, from which I lit out clad in furry dust that had been slumbering there for years.

I tried to stand up to it. When it was raining hard and it offered itself fallaciously to my hand, I tried to stay out in the rain in order to oblige it to get wet with me. Then, another rascality, it never missed the opening of a drain, a gap in the pavement or the conduit of a gutter, and, introducing its iron tip slyly into the crack, the fissure or the hole, it allowed itself to bend momentarily, curving elastically, and, straightening abruptly like a spring, it bounded backwards into the face of a passer-by, who launched furiously into nasty imprecations, or it went to lie down in the gutter, sticky with mud and filth, where it disappeared entirely.

Determined to prevail, I gathered one day in a corner my fire-tongs, my umbrella and my cane and tied them together solidly, certain that the perverse individual could not, by itself, drag the others into the depths of the mysterious lairs where it was accustomed to hide. A week of forced imprisonment might perhaps reason with the acrobat.

Well, my cane didn't budge, it's true; every evening, when I came home, I found it on its chain, true again; but in contact with it, my honest umbrella became gangrenous. Its cap no longer opens; on its struts, suddenly rusted by a damp without any apparent cause, the silk ripped with a click the first time I tried to open it. As for my tongs, it is in vain that I set them upright every evening in the corner of the fireplace; every night, regularly, they fall over with a frightful clatter that wakes me up with a start, they populate my slumber with alarming nightmares full of grimacing phantoms dragging chains . . .

Today, I declare myself vanquished by it. I'm afraid of it!

THOSE WHO DANCE

DISHEVELED or correct; Bullier or high society drawing-rooms; black coat and waist-coat or casual wear; low necklines under candlelight or skirts tucked up under gaslight shining on bright stockings and multicolored garters; arrogance here, gaiety there; high collars open at the cleavage, musky, made-up and powdered, or closed corsages and bare calves.

Two great categories, in consequence.

There, gentlemen disguised as people going mad, to use the witty expression of the unforgettable Gavarni;[1] stiff dances to a slow rhythm; long and broad formal steps; hands that scarcely touch; waists one dares not grasp, for fear of breaking one's dancing partner in two, who is overflowing her corset above and below; here, fantastic cavaliers, audacious entrechats, stupefy-ing exchanges, enlacements of arms and intersections

---

1 The illustrator "Paul Gavarni" (Sulpice Chevalier, 1804-1866), notable for his caricaturish depictions of Opéra balls.

of thighs during vertiginous waltzes, legs within arm's reach showing their plump calves in the pell-mell of whirling quadrilles.

There, glacially stern faces and constrained, stereotypical, identical smiles and simpers studied at length in advance in a mirror; here, trumpeting bursts of voices, deafening appeals, overlapping howls, flying insults whose mouths are rackets that send them back from one end of the room to the other, with cascades of laughter that roll and reverberate in the corners.

And those people are all amusing themselves in their fashion. Alongside them there are others; there are:

THOSE WHO WATCH
DANCING

A group of philosophers; not very numerous and quite different, in accordance with the environment in which people are dancing: high society drawing-rooms or Bullier—I am still taking the two extremes.

Here, to begin with, are old dowagers with white corkscrew curls, old dowagers who are doing tapestry and whispering in one another's ear, between two compliments on the grace of their respective daughters, stories of their past.

"Do you remember, Baronne . . . ?"

"Oh, Marquise, how distant all that is beginning to be!"

And, melancholy, they pull the petals from the tea-roses of distant memories, watching themselves live again in their little daughters, those paltry virgins with sharp elbows, stifling in their whalebone, sketching correct steps with distracted expressions, the decency of which is imposed less by usage than by their dress, which shackles their legs, and their outrageously tightened corset, which causes the chlorotic blood that they still have in the heart to rise to their wan faces.

At the Bullier it's something else. A hedge has formed around the quadrille, where the pale fat woman suddenly flattens out in splits of the utmost chic.

Here is the young student playing truant, the beardless college boy who has put on civilian dress in order to look like a man. He has used their elbows in order to place himself in the front rank of the curious and, his gaze wide-eyed, moist and lit up behind the lorgnon cavalierly camped on his nose, he is hypnotized by the women's legs casually exhibited, intoxicated by the wind of skirts that whip his face and make frissons of lubricity run down his back. Then, further away, there again is the mocking old student smoking his pipe leaning on a column. He is blasé with regard to all that display of white petticoats and more or less striped stockings—he has seen so many—and if he comes to the Bullier it is as an observer, to watch those who watch and to amuse himself surprising, here and there, in the eyes of the young ones, the fugitive glimmer, the gleam of desire that he too recalls having caused to quiver, some ten years ago, when he was a first year student.

ADVICE

"Stupid! That is," he said, "the epithet that best fits women.

"By virtue of hearing nonsense talked by the imbeciles who lure them, with the objective you know, convinced that one doesn't catch flies with vinegar, women have ended up adding faith to the compliments, too interested to be true, with which they are showered, to wit: firstly, that they are the fair sex; secondly, that they have a finesse that men lack; thirdly, that men have a heap of duties to fulfill in their regard, synthesized under the vocable *gallantry*.

"All that is absurd. Ninety-nine times out of a hundred they are ugly and lack flair. The intelligent man who knows how to live will roll over, without her suspecting it, the most cunning of women, *if he has no need to*. And as for gallantry, it's quite simply a tactic of war.

"You want a woman; you lay siege to her.

"Gallantry is the commencement of hostilities

"And the silly fool takes that for a duty that is being rendered to her.

"Let's see, on due reflection, which is the dupe here and which is the duper.

"Will the woman play eternally in life the role of the crow in the fable? Will she never perceive, that perspicacious individual, that it is only in view of the cheese that the fox praises her plumage?

"Now I, who don't like cheese, feel no inclination to play the role of the fox.

"Another reason that exasperates me against woman is the conclusion that she draws from her pretended superiority; the disdain that she has for men and the scant credit that she gives them in general—for in particular, once a strong man has imposed himself, the disdainful woman becomes supple; she is subjugated.

"See, for example how she takes possession of the sidewalk when she is walking there. Wouldn't one think that it's entirely hers? When she is alone she strides along, looking busy, her gaze attached to the toes of her ankle boots, for fear of the brisk comment that sometimes stings her as she passes by, alarming her conventional modesty. But when there are two or three they become bold, lining up complaisantly, obstructing the circulation, elbowing and jostling with the air of outraged queens the pitiful pedestrian who doesn't get out of the way quickly enough.

"So, my great distraction is to go forth in the populous streets, to oppose my vast stature to their shouldering, which scrapes against me. I never move aside, and as they expect—always the routine—that I'll abandon the sidewalk to them, there are collisions entirely to their disadvantage, since they are intended on my part and unintended on theirs, impacts that bruise 'the snow of their breasts' under the satin of their dresses. It's necessary to see the glares that they direct at me and the cries of 'Brute!' with which they pepper me.

"But I pass on, pitiless and impassive, without descending from the sidewalk; I become elastic to impacts; I play the spiral spring; I am the jostler; I make my gap, welcoming with a sly tip of the hat the: 'There's one of them; one can see what he is,' that flows from pursed lips in an admirably scornful smile.

"The place where I operate most frequently is in big department stores like Bon Marché and the Louvre. There, a woman is so completely at home, and believes herself so strongly to have the right to reign alone, that she no longer sees a man, and marches over him as simply as if he were a rag. Then I shout loudly—they all have a horror of being remarked—'Hey, pay attention, Madame, you're treading on my toes!' I howl: 'Pardon me, but is there any means of getting by?' or even: 'Hey, tell me, don't disturb yourself, belly here and backside there—am I supposed to go underneath you?'

"And I can assure you that they get out of the way.

"It's in encounters on staircases, most of all, that it becomes comical. She's coming down, I'm going up, here we are nose to nose, two centimeters apart buccally speaking.

"It's only at the moment of impact when the shock makes her go 'oh!' and she sees me, suddenly looming up before her like a wall that it's absolutely necessary to go around. The shock is such that she can't find anything to say and contents herself, half-winded, in looking at me from the height of her step—but it's her who pivots.

"Outside, on rainy days, I walk along with my cane—I don't mind getting wet. Naturally, the sidewalk is full of little women who are trotting in pairs, tucked up, ad blocking the passage completely with their two umbrellas. If you're gallant you only have two alternatives: descend into the gutter—which is to say, soil your boots and splash your trousers—or flatten yourself along the wall; which is to say, get plaster on your back and, on the other hand, get your face scratched by the struts of an umbrella, for they don't give you any leeway at all.

"I, who take pride in being uncivil, insinuate myself tranquilly between them, moving aside one of the umbrellas with the tip of my cane, just enough for my head to pass through without encumbrance. Too bad if the feather of a hat is uncurled or the rain stains the velvet or the dark green otter-skin.

"And there, along with a thousand others, are a few means that I recommend to you for amusing yourself by annoying women."

LAST LEGS

"Legs are on the way out," observed the connoisseur of calves, dejectedly, "and the best proof is that women no longer tuck up their skirts. Look, my dear friend, it's starting to rain; the opportunity is particularly propitious, if you'd care to follow me."

And he took me to the Place Saint-Michel.

The terrace where we sat down, disdaining of the noisy "student youth," which fortunately doesn't extend that far, is veritably one of the most picturesque corners and the most conducive to blissfully contemplative reverie. Fatigued by the incessant glare of the trams and multicolored omnibuses that cross paths on the Place Saint-Michel, the gaze, inclining slightly to the right, can repose on the double line of plane trees, the pale green foliage of which plumes the parapets all the way to the Louvre, which serves as a backcloth to the scene.

That is why my subtle and delicate friend, the connoisseur of calves, took me there, and above all because, from the Pont Saint Michel, beaten at that moment by sudden squall, one can savor the foolish hope of seeing emerge at any moment, skirt in one hand and umbrella in the other, sprightly Parisiennes, artistically shod, whom the rain has surprised outdoors. And because, at the corner of the bridge, it is necessary for them, in order to reach the sidewalk where we were lying in wait, to traverse the end of the causeway of the Quai Saint-Michel, the mud of which, incessantly kneaded by the large wheels of the Villette-Saint-Sulpice, forces them to tuck up quite squarely the packet of white petticoats in order to preserve it from splashes. For the Parisienne, a sagely economical housekeeper, would rather get her stockings dirty than her petticoats, which is very fortunate for the last connoisseurs of the last calves.

Oh yes, the last calves. For, as my friend had so justly deplored—and who ought one to blame for that heartbreaking state of things?—legs are on the way out.

What will henceforth provide fodder for our eyes, we poor folk who only find the female leg adorable— we whose gaze marveled to see along the boulevards the gamut of ladies' colored stockings fluttering, in the times, already distant, when the dust was, like the rain, a pretext for them to display those riches to the eyes of fond men?

Alas! Now the long tibias and fibulas are emaciating and their muscles withering; now, in high-heeled boots thin legs are wedged, around which corkscrew desolating stockings that don't even sustain the slightest suspicion of a calf. And bloomers are getting longer, in order to veil those miseries, and petticoats, once so brazenly puffed out, are now hanging down, pitiful and lamentable, as if they were ashamed of allowing the poverties they hide to be seen.

Alas, alas! The connoisseur of calves is right: legs are on the way out!

A PARTIAL LIST OF SNUGGLY BOOKS

A PARTIAL LIST OF SNUGGLY BOOKS

CPSIA information can be obtained
at www.ICGtesting.com
Printed in the USA
LVHW030349120620
657889LV00022B/3554

9 781645 250289